Praise for

◀ THE KIDS OF THE POLK STREET SCHOOL

"The stories have a natural air about them. Beginning readers should find themselves easily involved in these 'real' books."

—*Booklist*

"Sims's drawings dance with energy." —*Publishers Weekly*

Patricia Reilly Giff is the author of many beloved books for children, including the Kids of the Polk Street School books, the Friends and Amigos books, and the Polka Dot Private Eye books.

Several of her novels for older readers have been chosen as ALA Notable Books and ALA Best Books for Young Adults. They include *The Gift of the Pirate Queen; All the Way Home; Nory Ryan's Song,* a Society of Children's Book Writers and Illustrators Golden Kite Honor Book for Fiction; *Maggie's Door;* and the Newbery Honor Books *Lily's Crossing* and *Pictures of Hollis Woods. Lily's Crossing* was also chosen as a *Boston Globe–Horn Book* Honor Book. Her most recent book is *A House of Tailors.* Patricia Reilly Giff lives in Connecticut.

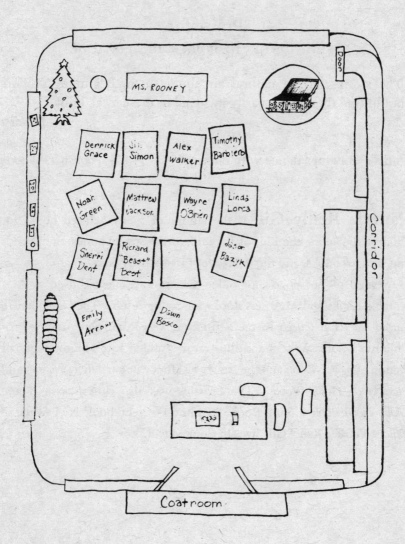

December Secrets

Patricia Reilly Giff

Illustrated by Blanche Sims

SCHOLASTIC INC.

New York   Toronto   London   Auckland   Sydney
Mexico City   New Delhi   Hong Kong   Buenos Aires

ISBN-13: 978-0-439-89507-1
ISBN-10: 0-439-89507-3

23 22   15 16/0

Printed in the U.S.A.   40

First Scholastic printing, December 2006

Chapter 1

Emily Arrow bit down on her pencil. Then she started to write.

> **The firefighter is your friend.**
> **He puts out fires.**
> **He comes to school.**
> **He takes you for a ride in his turk.**

Something didn't look right.

Emily raised her hand.

"How do you spell *truck*?" she asked Ms. Rooney.

"Good question, Emily," said Ms. Rooney. She wrote *truck* on the blackboard.

"The fire truck is in the schoolyard," Emily whispered to her friend Richard Best. "I can hear the sirens, Beast."

"Me too," Beast said. He was drawing a big red fire truck.

Right then the firefighter was giving another class a ride.

One of the kids would be sitting up in the front with the firefighter, Emily thought. He'd be wearing the big black fire hat. He'd be ringing the siren.

Ms. Rooney's class would be next.

Emily hoped she'd be in the front, wearing the big hat, ringing the siren.

She was wearing her almost-new pink sweatsuit. It had dark blue polka dots and a little green stain on one knee.

She hoped no one would see the green stain.

When they walked out to the fire truck, she was going to keep her knees together.

She looked around. Dawn Bosco was wearing a brand-new sweatsuit. It had a big *D* on the shirt. *D* for Dawn.

It should be *L* for Lucky, Emily thought.

Dawn Bosco always had the best stuff.

Even her middle name, Tiffanie, was great.

Her almost middle name.

Dawn's real middle name began with an *M*. But she'd never tell what it was.

Emily hoped it was something horrible.

"It's snowing out," shouted Beast.

Everyone ran to the window.

Jill Simon looked as if she were going to cry.

Jill always looked as if she were going to cry.

"Maybe we can't go out to the fire truck now," she said.

"Shh," Emily said. "Don't give Ms. Rooney any ideas."

Jill shook her head. She rubbed her eyes.

Emily looked at her for a minute.

Everything about Jill was fat. She had four fat braids. Two in front. Two in back. She was wearing four yellow loopy ribbons on her braids.

They made her head look like a round yellow sun.

But her face didn't look like the sun, Emily thought. Her face looked like a big fat raincloud.

"Time to go outside," Ms. Rooney said. "Bundle up. It's cold out there."

Emily bundled up. She wished she had a long jacket. Long enough to cover the green stain on her knee.

She took Uni, her white rubber unicorn, out of her desk. She tucked him in her pocket.

She raced to get near the front of the line.

She made sure she ran with her knees bent. It made her jacket look longer.

She hoped the firefighter would see her up in front. She hoped he'd ask her to sit in the seat with him and wear the fire hat.

Dawn Bosco tapped her on the arm. "Can I get ahead of you, Emily?" she asked.

The line started down the hall. Emily made believe she hadn't heard Dawn. She hurried as fast as she could with her knees bent.

In back of her everyone was bunching up.

4

Everyone wanted to get near the front.

"Can I—" Dawn started to ask again.

Outside Ms. Rooney clapped her hands. "We're not going to a fire," she said.

The firefighter laughed. She was a woman.

She helped Beast and Matthew Jackson climb up on the side of the truck. Emily was next.

Dawn quickly moved in front of Emily.

"Hey," Emily said.

But the firefighter put Dawn up on the side of the truck.

"You're next," she said to Emily.

"Can I sit in the front?" she asked.

"Why not?" she said. She let Emily climb up into the front seat.

Jill Simon started to cry.

"What's the matter?" the firefighter asked.

"I wanted to sit in front," Jill said.

Big baby, Emily wanted to say.

"Plenty of room," the firefighter said. "Move over a little," she told Emily.

Emily moved over an inch.

Jill squeezed in next to her. "Can I wear the hat too?" she asked the firefighter.

"Hey," Emily said. "I—"

The firefighter put the big black hat on Jill. She swung into the seat.

Emily looked at Jill.

Jill looked big and fat with the hat on her head.

She looked silly with all those yellow ribbons hanging out under the hat.

Emily looked down. She could see the stain on her knee. It looked very green.

She sighed. She'd have to wait a whole year before the fire truck came back to the Polk Street School. She'd have to wait another year for a chance at the fire hat.

Chapter 2

"That was really exciting," Ms. Rooney said when they were back in the classroom. "Everyone's cheeks are red."

Emily's hands still felt cold. She blew on them a little.

"It's the first day of December," Ms. Rooney said. She looked at the class. "Does anyone know what happens in December?"

Noah Green raised his hand. "It's Hanukkah."

"Right," said Ms. Rooney. She drew a candle-holder on the board. It had one big candle in the middle and four smaller ones on each side.

"This is a special sign for Hanukkah," Ms. Rooney said. "It's called a menorah."

Matthew raised his hand. "It's Christmastime too."

Ms. Rooney nodded. She drew a green wreath

on the board. "And this is a special sign for Christmas."

Emily wished she knew something that happened in December.

Beast raised his hand. "One of our presidents had a birthday in December," he said.

"Very good," said Ms. Rooney. "Woodrow Wilson was born in December. He was our twenty-eighth president." She drew a flag on the blackboard. "President Andrew Johnson was born in December too."

Emily looked at Richard. She wondered how he knew about the presidents' birthdays.

Ms. Rooney asked Richard, "How did you know?"

Beast laughed. "I didn't. I just took a guess."

Emily tried to think of something to guess.

"I'll tell you something," Ms. Rooney said. "It's the month that someone patented chewing gum." She drew a square piece of pink chewing gum on the board.

Emily put her hand up in the air. At least she could ask what *patented* meant. It sounded like shiny shoes.

Ms. Rooney smiled at Emily. "Patent," she said. "When you invent something, you tell the government. Then no one else can say they invented it first."

Ms. Rooney looked at the big clock on the wall. "It's almost time for art," she said. "So I'll have to tell you this quickly."

She drew a line under the menorah and the wreath. "This is the time for giving," she said. "It's a special time for making other people happy. And that's what we'll do in the classroom."

"Presents?" asked Matthew.

"Yes," Ms. Rooney said. "But we'll do it in a special way. Everyone will pick one person in the classroom. He will be your secret friend. And all through December you can do special things for that person. You can draw pictures for him."

11

Timothy Barbiero said, "You can hide candy in his desk."

"Nice," said Ms. Rooney.

Dawn put her hand up. "You can pick up her book if she drops it."

"That's the spirit, Dawn," Ms. Rooney said.

Emily tried to think of something to say so that Ms. Rooney would say "That's the spirit" to her too. She raised her hand.

"Yes, Emily?"

Emily couldn't think of one thing to say. "I forgot," she told Ms. Rooney.

"Think of someone to pick," Ms. Rooney said. "Don't tell that person. Tell me."

Timothy raised his hand. "You mean, that person will never know?" he asked. "I have to give him stuff and he won't even know it's me?"

"Oh, yes," said Ms. Rooney. "Everyone will tell his secret friend on the last day of school before the winter vacation."

She held up her hand. "But it doesn't have to cost money. Do nice things for your secret person."

Ms. Rooney looked at the clock again. "One more thing," she said. "Tomorrow bring a box. Bring a cigar box. Or maybe a writing-paper box. We're going to do something exciting with it."

Ms. Rooney smiled. "Time for art now."

The class lined up.

Emily looked around at everyone.

Beast was at the end of the line. His head was way back. His pink eraser was sitting on top of his nose.

Beast was a very funny boy.

She'd pick Beast for her special person.

She tried to think of ways to make him happy.

Beast loved to draw.

Emily had an almost-new box of crayons. All of the points were sharp.

Except for the red crayon.

That's because red was her favorite. It was also

because she had drawn lots of red turkeys last month.

She'd give Beast the box of almost-new crayons.

All of them except for the red one.

The class marched into the art room.

Emily took her seat. Maybe Beast wouldn't see that the red crayon was missing.

"Guess what month this is?" asked Mrs. Kara.

"December," everyone yelled.

"Very good," said Mrs. Kara. She passed out drawing paper. "How about drawing some December things?"

Emily took her crayon box out of the art cubby.

She pulled out a yellow crayon. She'd make a big candleholder like the one Ms. Rooney had drawn.

Matthew poked her in the back. "Can I borrow a green crayon?" he asked.

She passed it back to him.

"Guess what?" he said. "I'm going to pick Beast for my secret person."

Emily frowned.

"He's my best friend," Matthew said. "He invited me to his Thanksgiving sleep-over last week. It was the best party in the world."

"Oh," Emily said. She drew nine sticks for candles. She put big orange flames on them.

She tried to think of someone else to pick for that special person.

Dawn Bosco leaned over. She looked at Emily's picture. "That's very nice, Emily," she said.

Emily smiled at her. Maybe she should pick Dawn.

Emily looked at Dawn's picture. Dawn had drawn a picture of a girl. She had a great big pink chewing-gum bubble coming out of her mouth.

"I like your picture too," Emily said.

Dawn smiled. She drew a pink sweatsuit on the girl. She put blue polka dots on the sweatsuit.

"Hey, that's me," Emily said.

Dawn picked up a green crayon. She drew a little green mark on the girl's pink sweatsuit. She drew it right on the knee. "How come you didn't let me get ahead of you in line?" she asked.

Emily looked at the green mark. She didn't answer.

Mrs. Kara clapped her hands. "Hold up your drawings," she told the class. She looked around. "Just lovely."

Emily ducked her head. She hoped Mrs. Kara didn't know that Dawn's picture was supposed to be Emily.

Emily certainly wouldn't pick Dawn for her secret person. She'd have to pick someone else.

Chapter 3

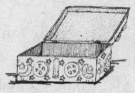

Wayne O'Brien was a nice boy, Emily thought. Maybe she would pick him.

Wayne liked fish a lot.

She could cut out fish pictures. She could draw fish in a bowl. She could buy fish food so he could feed the class fish, Drake and Harry.

Wayne was a perfect special December person.

Emily waited until the bell rang. Everyone lined up to go home. They raced out the door.

Emily went up to Ms. Rooney's desk. "I picked a secret person," she said.

"Nice, Emily," said Ms. Rooney. She pulled out a notebook. "I'm writing down all the secret persons. That way, no one will get left out."

"My secret person will be Wayne," Emily said.

Ms. Rooney looked at her book. "Sorry, Emily. Someone chose Wayne already."

"Oh," Emily said. "I was going to pick Beast, but—"

Ms. Rooney shook her head. "Someone picked him too."

Emily looked at all the desks. She tried to picture who sat at each one.

Should she pick Sherri Dent? No.

Linda Lorca? Not really.

"How about Dawn?" Ms. Rooney said.

Emily thought about the green stain. She thought about Dawn's picture. She shook her head. "No."

Ms. Rooney looked at her book again. "I have a perfect secret person for you," she said.

"Who?"

"Jill."

"Jill Simon?" Emily asked.

Ms. Rooney smiled. "That's the only Jill we have."

Emily smiled too. She shook her head a little.

Jill was a crybaby. A fat crybaby.

And fat crybabies were no fun.

"Yes," said Ms. Rooney. "I think Jill would be a good secret person. And she could use a friend."

Emily looked out the window. There were a few dots of snow coming down. "I guess I'll pick Matthew."

Ms. Rooney looked down at her book. "Oh, dear," she said. "Someone picked Matthew."

Emily looked at the snow again.

Maybe she could be her own secret person, she thought. She could save her own money. She could buy herself some nice bags of chocolate candy.

She could buy herself a pretty notebook. A blue one with pink flowers. Nicer than the one Dawn had.

She cleared her throat. "Did anyone pick herself?"

Ms. Rooney looked a little shocked. "No," she said.

Emily made herself look a little shocked too. "That wouldn't be very nice, would it?"

Ms. Rooney shook her head. "No."

"No," Emily said too. She looked up at the ceiling. "Who's left?"

"Jill Simon."

Emily sighed. "All right," she said. "I guess Jill will be my secret person."

Emily zipped her jacket. Then she went outside.

Beast was standing in front. He was trying to scoop up snow from the grass.

"Not too much snow," Emily said.

Beast shook his head.

"What are you doing here?" Emily asked.

"Waiting for my sister, Holly. She takes forever."

"Who's your secret person?" Emily asked.

Beast looked around. "Matthew," he whispered. "Who's yours?"

Emily looked around too. "It's Jill Simon."

Beast grabbed his throat. He fell on the grass. "Yucko," he said.

"Jill is a very nice girl," Emily said. "She could really use a friend."

"She could really use a diet," Beast said.

Emily nodded. "What are you going to do first for your secret person?"

Beast stuck out his finger and caught a snowflake. "My father has some after-shave stuff," he said. "He never uses it. I think he'll give it to me for Matthew."

"Matthew shaves?" Emily asked, surprised.

Beast shook his head. "No, he still wets the bed a little. I thought he could put on some of the after-shave stuff. It would make him smell better."

"That's a good idea," Emily said.

She started down the path.

Beast was lucky to have such a good idea.

It was hard to think of something to do for Jill.

Emily walked around a telephone pole. Too bad Jill was such a fat crybaby.

Maybe she could do something to make Jill skinny and happy.

What a wonderful December thing that would be.

She had some magazines at home. She started to run. She knew just what she was going to do.

Chapter 4

The next morning it was raining.

In school Emily hung up her yellow raincoat. She put her pink and green writing-paper box on the shelf.

She took the two magazine pictures out of the Baggie her mother had given her.

"Hi, Emily," Ms. Rooney said. "You're early."

"Yes." Emily held up her pictures. "I have a present for my secret person."

"Wonderful," Ms. Rooney said. She put her umbrella in the coatroom. "Aren't you sorry it didn't snow?"

"I've been wishing for snow all week," Emily said. She smoothed out her two pictures. Then she tiptoed over to Jill's desk.

Before she put the pictures on Jill's seat, she took a look at them.

One was a picture of a baby. The baby was fat. She was wearing a diaper.

She looked a lot like Jill. Except she was smiling.

On the bottom of the picture Emily had written *Smile*.

She had written it with her best red crayon. Her best red crayon with the yucko point.

It was a little hard to tell that the writing said *Smile*.

She had cut the other picture from a summer magazine. It showed a green cabbage and a yellow squash.

Emily hadn't written anything on the bottom.

She hoped that Jill Simon would think about eating things that would make her skinny.

Emily could hear children coming down the hall.

She put the pictures on Jill's seat. Then she went back to her own desk.

Up in front Ms. Rooney had taken a bunch

26

of plastic Baggies out of a big brown paper bag.

The Baggies were filled with white things.

Just then Beast came into the classroom.

So did Noah and Dawn.

Beast ran to Matthew's desk. He put a bottle on Matthew's seat.

It was half filled with green liquid.

Then Beast slid into his own seat.

Emily wished Jill would hurry.

Jill would be so happy when she saw Emily's pictures.

The bell rang.

The rest of the children came into the classroom. All except for Jill.

Matthew took off his jacket. Then he looked at the bottle on his seat. He took the cap off and smelled it. "Phew," he said.

Emily looked at Beast. She hoped he didn't feel bad.

27

But Beast was bent over his desk. He was drawing a picture of a Christmas tree.

Jill came into the classroom at last.

She had on a big blue plastic rainhat. It looked like the kind of hat Emily's mother wore in the shower.

Jill took her hat off and shook the rain out of it.

She was wearing four white ribbons on her four fat braids.

She looked like a snowball, Emily thought.

A big, fat white snowball.

Jill had a brown paper bag with her.

Emily smiled to herself.

It was probably a present for Jill's secret person.

Emily wondered who her secret person was.

Jill went to her seat. She sat right on top of Emily's two secret person pictures.

At the front of the room Ms. Rooney clapped her hands.

"We're going to do something special today," she told the class. "Something special for December."

Emily looked at Jill. She wondered if Jill would ever stand up so she could see her secret person present.

"Who can tell us the story of Hanukkah?" Ms. Rooney asked.

Noah put his hand up. "Once upon a time there was a good queen. Her name was Esther, I think. And then there was a very bad man. His name was—"

Jill Simon raised her hand. She stood up.

Emily leaned over to see what had happened to the pictures.

The picture of the baby was wrinkled on the edge.

"I think that's wrong, Ms. Rooney," Jill said in a soft voice. "Noah's mixed up. He's telling the story of Purim. He's supposed to be telling the story of the oil."

"No, I'm not," said Noah.

Then he put his hand up to his mouth. "I guess you're right," he said. He made a face at Jill.

"I'm just trying to help," Jill said. She sounded as if she were going to cry.

Jill sat down again without looking at her chair.

Emily sat back. She watched Jill open the brown paper bag.

Jill reached in. She took out a chocolate chip cookie. Then she ducked down behind a book so Ms. Rooney wouldn't see her. She took a bite of the cookie.

"Hanukkah," said Noah. "Well. Once upon a time the Jews had to fight for their freedom. Then they won. They wanted to light the temple light."

Ms. Rooney pointed to the menorah on the blackboard. She nodded at Noah.

"But there was only enough oil to keep the temple lamp lit for one day."

Jill raised her hand. "Let me tell the rest."

Noah sighed. "Go ahead."

"Very thoughtful, Noah," Ms. Rooney said.

"Even though there wasn't enough oil, the candle stayed lighted for eight days," Jill said.

"Now," said Noah, "we light a candle every night for eight nights."

"And we get a present every night for eight nights too," said Jill.

"Lucky," said Matthew.

Ms. Rooney held up one of the Baggies. "We're going to make presents," she said. "You may use them for Christmas or for Hanukkah."

Beast said, "I think it's time for gym now."

Ms. Rooney frowned. She looked at the clock. "Absolutely right, Richard. I guess we'll have to make our presents later."

The class lined up.

Emily watched until Jill stood up.

This time Jill saw the pictures.

They were all wrinkled.

31

Jill looked a little surprised. She looked at the pictures for a moment. Then she crumpled them up and put them into the wastebasket.

Emily gritted her teeth. Just her luck to get such a dummy for a secret December person.

Chapter 5

The next day, after Mrs. Paris's reading class, Emily went back to the science table. She looked at the fishbowl.

"Hi, Harry," she said to the striped fish.

She looked at Harry's eyes. They were always open. She wondered if Harry ever went to sleep.

Emily tried to keep her eyes open too.

She counted to thirty-four. Then she had to blink.

"Hi, Drake," she said to the other fish.

Drake was the mean one. He was always eating. He never gave Harry a chance.

Drake opened his mouth wide. Then he shut it. Pop.

Emily did the same thing.

Beast came back to the table. "Hi, Fish Face," he said to Emily.

Emily laughed.

Beast took a little fish food in his fingers.

He tried to drop it on Harry's side of the bowl.

But Drake swam over quickly. He opened his mouth to grab the food.

"Mean," said Beast.

"Did you get a present today?" Emily asked.

Beast shook his head. "No. Well, maybe."

"What—" Emily began.

"I found a Good and Plenty candy in my desk."

"That's not much," Emily said.

"No," said Beast. "And I had Good and Plentys last week. This one may have been left over. Did you get a present?"

Emily shook her head. "Not yet."

"I thought I saw someone put—" Beast began. Then he closed his mouth.

"In my desk?" Emily asked.

Beast pressed his lips together.

"Who was it?" Emily asked.

34

Beast covered his mouth with his hand. He shook his head. "Don't ask me," he said.

"All right, class," Ms. Rooney said. "It's time to start our December presents."

All the children raced back to their seats.

Emily reached into her desk. No present.

Ms. Rooney held up one of the Baggies. "Guess what I have?"

"Macaroni," someone said.

"Not just ordinary macaroni," Ms. Rooney said.

She held up some fat shells. She held up some short squiggly ones. Then she held up some wheels.

Emily stuck her head into her desk.

There was nothing special in the desk.

Maybe she was nobody's special December person.

"Take out your cigar boxes," Ms. Rooney said.

Emily went to the coatroom. She took her pink and green box off the shelf. Then she went back to her seat.

"Now," said Ms. Rooney. "Will our glue monitor give out the glue, please?"

Timothy Barbiero went to the front of the room.

He gave out the honey-colored jars of glue.

"This is easy," said Ms. Rooney. She held up a box.

"Ah," said everyone.

It was the most beautiful box Emily had ever seen. It was covered with macaroni. Macaroni shells. Macaroni wheels. Squiggly macaroni. Gold macaroni.

"How—" Beast started to ask.

"Gold spray paint," Ms. Rooney said. "I have gold spray and silver spray."

Dawn Bosco put her hand up.

So did Emily.

"I want gold," Dawn said.

Ms. Rooney frowned a little. "We're not up to that yet."

Emily quickly put her hand down.

"This is our December present," Ms. Rooney

said. She pointed to her box. "It will be ready for the first night of Hanukkah. If you celebrate Hanukkah, you may take it home to your mother and father. Or you may save it for a Christmas present."

"Hey," Dawn said. "Look at this." She held up a blue barrette. "It was in my desk."

Jill looked as if she were going to cry.

"I didn't get anything," Jill said.

Emily wanted to hit her right in her big, fat white snowball head. "You did so," she started to say.

Then she shut her mouth.

Jill turned around. "What did you say, Emily?"

"I said, I didn't get anything either," Emily said in a cross voice.

Ms. Rooney called Emily up to her desk. "You may pick a macaroni Baggie, Emily. Pour a few on everyone's desk."

Emily picked wheels.

She poured a few on everyone's desk.

She poured five on Beast's desk because he was her friend.

She poured only two on Jill Simon's desk because Jill had sat on her present.

She poured only one on Dawn Bosco's desk because she still remembered the green stain.

Some of the other children were walking around the room. They were putting macaroni on people's desks.

Matthew was giving out ziti.

Dawn was giving out stars.

"Hey," Emily said to Dawn. "How come you gave me only one star?"

Dawn put her shoulders up in the air. "How come you gave me only one wheel?"

Jill Simon started to cry. "I don't have enough."

Ms. Rooney sighed. "I have plenty for everyone."

Emily picked up her glue. She poured some on her box. Then she stuck a wheel in the middle.

39

She was going to hurry up. She was going to be the first one finished.

As soon as her box dried she was going to ask Ms. Rooney to spray it for her. Gold.

It was going to be the best box in the classroom.

And she'd keep it all for herself.

At least someone would think she was a secret December person.

Even though that person was just herself.

Chapter 6

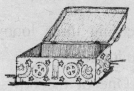

It was Wednesday. Time for music.

Emily gave Uni, her rubber unicorn, a gallop across her desk.

She took a look at the window. The macaroni boxes were lined up on the sill.

Hers was beautiful. It was sprayed with gold.

"Hurry, everyone," said Ms. Rooney.

Mrs. Avery was waiting for them in the music room. "Open your books to page twenty-one," she said. "We'll sing a Christmas song."

Emily looked outside. It was starting to snow.

It was starting to feel like Christmas. It was less than a week away.

She opened to page twenty-one.

The name of the song was "Rudolph the Red-nosed Reindeer."

Jill was sitting in front of Emily. She was

41

wearing three loopy red bows. She looked like Rudolph.

One of the bows must have fallen off, Emily thought.

She looked like a messy Rudolph.

The class began to sing.

Next to Emily, Dawn Bosco was singing. She was singing very loud.

She had a terrible voice. Screechy.

Emily tried to sing a little louder than Dawn. She knew her voice was nice.

Mrs. Avery always said so.

This time Mrs. Avery raised her eyebrows a little. "Dawn Bosco and Emily Arrow," she said. "How about singing a little softer? This is not a shouting match."

Beast and Matthew started to laugh. They made believe they were boxers fighting each other.

"That will do," Mrs. Avery told them.

Emily sang a little softer. She didn't have to look at her book.

Dawn had to look at her book.

Emily was glad she knew all the words by heart.

She turned the page to see what came next.

Someone had put a piece of paper inside her book. It was a picture of three girls. They were all wearing mittens.

Underneath someone had written in blue crayon:

Good Frineds

Emily looked around. She wondered who had put the picture in her book.

She turned the picture over. On the back someone had written:

Good frineds let peple ahead of them in line.

Emily crumpled the paper up. That Dawn Bosco.

What kind of a present was that to give to a good friend?

Emily marched up to the wastebasket.

She threw the crumpled up picture inside.

Mrs. Avery tapped on her desk. "Emily Arrow," she said. "Why did you get up in the middle of our song? You know better than that."

Emily didn't say anything.

She wanted to say that Dawn was the one who should know better.

Mrs. Avery frowned at her. "I think you'd better go back to your classroom. Tell Ms. Rooney that you are not interested in Christmas music."

Emily hurried out of the music room. She didn't want everybody to see that she had tears in her eyes.

She didn't want everyone to think she was a crybaby like Jill Simon.

Before she went back to her classroom, she stopped in the girls' room.

She could hear her class singing.

They were singing "It's Beginning to Look a Lot Like Christmas."

Emily looked in the mirror. Her face was red.

It was beginning to look as if she were going to have a terrible December.

Slowly she walked back to her classroom.

She hated to tell Ms. Rooney that Mrs. Avery had said she wasn't interested in Christmas music.

She was very interested in Christmas music.

She was practically the only one who knew all the words by heart.

Ms. Rooney was sitting at her desk. "What's the matter, Emily?" she asked.

Emily started to cry. "Dawn tried to get me in trouble."

"Really?" Ms. Rooney said.

"Yes," said Emily. She sniffed a little. She needed a tissue. "Dawn tried to sing louder than me."

Ms. Rooney passed her the hankie box.

Emily rubbed her nose. "Dawn doesn't want me for her secret December person either."

Ms. Rooney looked surprised. "Why do you think you're Dawn's secret person?"

"I guessed," Emily said.

Just then Matthew raced in.

He stopped when he saw Emily and Ms. Rooney. He put his hand over his mouth. "I didn't know anyone was here," he said.

"I'm here," said Ms. Rooney. "Why aren't you in music? Did you sing too loud too?"

"No." Matthew smiled. "I asked to go to the bathroom."

He reached into his pocket. He pulled out a box of Good and Plentys.

"I wanted to put this box of candy in Beast's desk."

"That's nice," said Ms. Rooney.

"Beast loves Good and Plentys," Matthew said. "Yesterday I bought him a box too." He put his shoulders up in the air. "I ate some before I got to school. I ate a lot."

Emily smiled at Matthew. It was hard not to eat Good and Plentys once you got started.

"I had only one left for Beast," Matthew said.

He put the box into Richard's desk. "But today I didn't eat many. Only six. I'm trying to get into the spirit of giving."

"That's lovely, Matthew," said Ms. Rooney.

"My mother said that's what should happen in December," Matthew said.

"Yes," said Emily. She wished Dawn would get into the spirit of giving.

She watched Matthew dash out of the classroom again. Then she went back to sit at her desk.

Chapter 7

It was hard to think of things to give Jill Simon.

Last night Emily had looked through her closet.

She had pulled out a pile of stuff. Shells from the beach last summer. Her old first-grade notebook.

At last she had found something.

A pencil.

It was a special pencil. Green. Her Aunt Helen had brought it back from California. It had a big, fat almost-new eraser.

It was long and very skinny.

Maybe it would make Jill think about being skinny. Maybe it would make Jill think about a diet.

When Emily got to the classroom, she looked at the pencil again. Jill would love it.

But she might not think about being skinny when she looked at it.

49

Ms. Rooney clapped her hands. "Today we're going to talk about Christmas."

Emily loved to talk about Christmas. She closed her eyes for a minute. She could see the Christmas tree in her living room. She could see presents.

She looked at the pencil again.

Maybe she should write a little note with it. A note to remind Jill about a diet.

"Who would like to tell us about Christmas?" Ms. Rooney asked.

Quickly Emily raised her hand.

Dawn Bosco's hand shot up in the air too.

Ms. Rooney called on Emily.

"Christmas," said Emily slowly. "It's surprises. And a tree. It's getting lots of presents."

Dawn waved her hand around. "It's not just getting presents," she said. "It's giving presents. That's the important thing."

"That's what my mother said," Matthew told the class.

Emily made a face at Dawn. She wanted to

say "I was going to tell about the giving part next."

She wished she had thought of it.

But Ms. Rooney was talking now. "Who can tell us more?" she asked.

Beast stood up. "It's a birthday. A special birthday. It's the day Jesus Christ was born."

"Exactly right," said Ms. Rooney.

Exactly right, thought Emily. She felt cross with herself. Too bad she hadn't thought about saying that.

She sighed. She looked at the pencil for Jill again.

Maybe she would write a poem to go with Jill Simon's secret December present.

What went with skinny? Minny. Jinny. Linny.

You won't look tinny when you're skinny.

No.

How about something with diet? Fi-et. Ly-et.

She thought for a minute.

How about:

A skinny dress your mother will buy it.
If you go on a diet.

That was a little better.

But not perfect.

She looked out the window. The snow had stopped.

How about:

Try a diet

Yes. That sounded good.

She said it in her head a couple of times. Try a diet. Try a diet.

Sherri Dent turned around. "Are you talking to yourself?" she whispered.

Emily shook her head. Then she took out her notebook. She tore out a piece of paper.

Ms. Rooney stopped talking about Christmas.

"Who is making that ripping noise?" she asked.

53

Emily ducked down.

"Yes," said Ms. Rooney after a minute. "We are very lucky. Mr. Mancina, the principal, is giving us a present. Our own class Christmas tree."

Everybody clapped.

Emily clapped too. Then she frowned.

Try a diet was no good.

It would hurt Jill's feelings. She might cry for an hour.

No. She peeked at Jill to be sure she wasn't looking at her.

Then she wrote *Surprise* on the piece of paper.

She wrote it with the long, skinny green pencil.

"We're going to make Christmas ornaments this week," said Ms. Rooney. "For the tree."

Everyone smiled. Beast was smiling the hardest.

Emily looked over at him. Beast loved to draw. He'd make a great ornament.

She reached into her desk for Uni, her rubber unicorn. Maybe she'd give him a run.

She pulled him out. He was wrapped up in paper.

Emily pulled the paper off.

Underneath he had a piece of red shiny material covering him.

A little card said:

A blanket for Uni

Next to her Dawn Bosco was playing with a piece of gum.

She saw Emily looking at her.

She pulled the gum into a long string.

Emily smiled.

Dawn blinked. Then she smiled back.

Emily gave Uni a pat. She could feel his new red cover. It felt smooth, beautiful.

She was sorry she hadn't let Dawn ahead of her on the fire-truck line.

She'd have to make it up to Dawn.

She waited until everyone lined up for lunch.

Quickly she put the pencil on Jill's desk.

Then she marched out the door.

Chapter 8

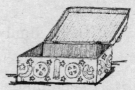

Emily reached into her desk. She felt the package.

Her mouth watered.

Inside the package were two cookies. Two big fat ones. Two sugar cookies with nuts and raisins and rainbow sprinkles on top.

She and her mother had made them last night.

These cookies were not for her secret December person. They were for Dawn Tiffanie Bosco.

As soon as Dawn got up to sharpen her pencil, Emily put the cookies inside her desk.

Then she sat back and waited.

Now Dawn would know she was sorry about the fire-truck line.

"I need some people to go on a message," Ms. Rooney said.

Emily raised her hand as hard as she could.

"All right, Emily," said Ms. Rooney. "You may go. And also . . ."

Beast knelt up on his seat.

He had a magnifying glass in his hand.

"Please, Ms. Rooney . . ." he began.

"Jill," said Ms. Rooney.

Beast slid down in his seat. He held his thumb up to the magnifying glass.

Emily smiled.

Beast had Matthew's old magnifying glass. It must be a secret December person present.

Emily went quickly to Ms. Rooney's desk.

"Go to the custodian's room," Ms. Rooney said. "Ask Jim to bring up the Christmas tree."

"Ooh," everyone said.

Emily hurried out of the room.

She was lucky. This was a terrific message.

She waited for Jill outside the door.

Today Jill was wearing green bows on her braids.

She looked like a fat green lollipop, Emily thought.

Emily remembered Jill was her secret December person. "Your bows look pretty," she said.

She crossed her fingers behind her back.

"Do you think so?" Jill asked. She took a little hop down the first step. "I think I look like a frog. A fat green frog." She hopped down the next step. *"Glunk, glunk."*

Emily's mouth opened.

Jill reached the bottom step. *"Glunk, glunk,"* she said again. She started to laugh a little.

Emily laughed a little too. Jill really looked funny with her braids jumping up and down.

"Do you think we could stop for water?" Jill asked. "I'm dying of thirst."

"A quick drink," Emily said.

"Yes," Jill said.

Emily took three gulps of water. *"Glunk, glunk,"* she said. "I sound just like a frog."

Jill laughed.

Emily waited while Jill took three gulps of water.

Jill didn't look like a fat green lollipop when she laughed.

Her face made Emily smile. It looked like the happy faces Beast drew in his notebook.

They stopped to look out the window.

"I wish it would snow," Jill said.

"Me too," Emily said. "We could sled right across the yard."

"Slide right into the flagpole," Jill said.

Emily laughed, thinking about people banging into the flagpole.

They knocked on Jim's door.

"Could we have the Christmas tree?" Emily asked. "For Room 113."

"Please," Jill added.

"Why not?" Jim said. He had a box of crackers in his hand. "Want some?"

Emily said, "Yes." She took one.

Jill said "Yes" too. She took two.

Then they ran upstairs again.

"I'm dying of hunger," Emily said.

"Me too," Jill said. She broke off part of her second cracker. She gave it to Emily.

Suddenly Emily remembered Dawn's cookies. She wondered if Dawn had found them.

"Let's hurry," she told Jill.

They raced down the hall.

Back in the classroom everyone was working on ornaments.

There was colored paper on everyone's desk. And pieces of ribbon and lace.

"Wow," said Emily when she went back to her desk.

Jill raised her hand. "I don't know how to do it." She looked as if she were going to cry.

Emily sighed. Jill looked like a raincloud again.

"Alex will help you," Mrs. Rooney told Jill.

Emily slid down in her seat.

She could see the cookies in Dawn's desk.

She wished Dawn would find them.

Emily went to her art cubby. She took out her scissors. She held them by the ears.

Ms. Rooney always made a big fuss if someone didn't carry his scissors by the ears.

Emily was so busy remembering how to hold her scissors that she didn't remember her crayons.

She went back to get them.

Ms. Rooney frowned. "Settle down, Emily."

Emily rushed back to her seat.

She cut out a big blue circle.

Then she looked for her glue.

The glue monitor had forgotten her.

She thought about getting up to get some. But Ms. Rooney would tell her to settle down again.

Maybe she'd draw some pictures on the blue ball first. Too bad the red crayon was yucko.

She reached for her crayon box.

"Hey," said Dawn. She pulled out the cookies. "Gorgeous," she said.

Emily looked over.

"Aren't they gorgeous?" Dawn said.

Emily nodded a little. She smiled at Dawn.

Dawn took a big bite. "I wonder who keeps giving me all this stuff?"

"I—" Emily began.

Dawn held up her hand. "Don't tell me. I want to be surprised on the last day of school."

Emily looked down at her crayon box. That Dawn Bosco. She knew very well who had made those cookies. She knew that Emily had baked them with her mother.

That mean Dawn Bosco.

She was making believe the cookies were a secret December person present.

Emily made a face at her.

Dawn stuck her tongue out at Emily.

Emily reached for her red crayon.

It wasn't hers. It was a brand-new one.

Emily put her hand over her mouth.

Dawn had given her a new red crayon.

She leaned over. "Dawn," she said. "Would you like to use my red crayon?"

Dawn stuck her tongue out at Emily again. "No, thank you very much," she said. "I have my own."

Then Dawn put the rest of the cookies into her mouth.

Chapter 9

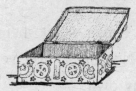

Emily rushed down the hall.

She had a secret December person present for Jill. It was the last one.

Today was the last day of school before the holidays. Noah had told her that Hanukkah began tonight. And Christmas was in two days.

Today was going to be a very exciting day.

Jill's mother was coming to school. She was giving the class potato pancakes for a Hanukkah treat. *"Latkes,"* Jill called them. She said they were wonderful.

Emily had a little box in her schoolbag.

Inside the box were four pink ribbons. They were for Jill's braids.

They would make Jill look like a fat pink pillow. So what?

Jill would look like a nice fat pink pillow.

Emily thought about the other day. She thought about Jill saying *"Glunk, glunk."* She thought about Jill sharing her cracker.

Emily quickly opened her schoolbag.

Ms. Rooney came into the room. "Good morning."

Emily said hello to Ms. Rooney. She put Jill's present inside her desk. Then she raced to her seat.

Dawn slid into the seat next to Emily. She put a package on her desk.

Emily looked at it out of the corner of her eye.

She knew it was for her.

It was a secret December person present.

She smiled at Dawn.

Dawn smiled back at her. "Let's be friends again."

"All right," Emily said.

"How do you like this?" Dawn asked. She pointed to the package.

"Very pretty," Emily said. She wondered

what was inside. She hoped it was something she liked.

Dawn leaned over. "It's a truck."

"A truck?" Emily said.

"It's for my secret person," Dawn said. "It's for Timothy Barbiero."

Dawn went over to stand in the pencil-sharpener line.

Emily took her pencil. She went to stand in line too. "How come you gave me the picture?" she asked Dawn.

"What picture?" Dawn asked.

"The one with the girls and the mittens," Emily said. "And the green stain on the knee."

Dawn ducked her head. "I was mad at you. I'm sorry."

"It's all right," Emily said. "I guess."

Emily let Jill get in line in front of her. Jill had her long skinny special pencil with her.

"Do you like that pencil?" Emily asked.

"I love it," Jill said.

Emily wished she could tell Jill something.

She wished she could tell her that she looked a lot better when she was smiling.

Jill was turning out to be a good friend.

Emily leaned forward. "You look nice when you smile."

"Thank you," Jill said.

"I wish you would smile a lot," Emily said. "It makes you look pretty."

"*Glunk, glunk,*" Jill said.

They both started to laugh.

Jill sharpened her pencil. Emily sharpened hers too. Then they went to look at their gold macaroni boxes.

"I love mine," Jill said. She lifted the top to show Emily.

Inside she had colored the box with a blue crayon.

"Pretty," Emily said. She wished she had thought of coloring the inside of hers. "Maybe I'll color mine."

"Good idea," Jill said.

"I'll color mine red," Emily said.

"I was going to do that," Jill said. "Red is my favorite color."

Then Jill put the top back on the macaroni box.

She didn't put it back right. The top fell.

A macaroni shell fell off. So did a wheel.

Jill looked as if she were going to cry.

"Don't cry," Emily said quickly.

Jill tried to smile.

They went back to their seats.

Then Jill's mother came. She had a big box in her hand. "Careful," she said. "They're hot."

Emily took a potato *latke*. Mrs. Simon gave her a paper napkin with a snowflake on it.

The *latke* was wonderful.

Emily watched as Jill reached into her desk.

Jill pulled out the box of pink ribbons. She held them up for everyone to see.

Then Emily reached into her desk. She took out her box of crayons. She had a great idea.

She'd color the inside of her macaroni box. She'd color it red. Jill's favorite color.

Then she'd give the box to Jill. She'd get her mother something else.

She took another potato *latke*.

She wondered why Jill hadn't colored the inside of her box red.

Maybe she didn't have a red crayon.

Emily took a deep breath.

"Hey," she said to Dawn. "I just thought of something."

Dawn looked up.

"If I'm not your secret December person," she said, "then who gave me a red crayon?"

"I can't tell," Dawn said.

Ms. Rooney clapped her hands. She stood in front of the class Christmas tree.

It looked beautiful. Everyone's ornament was hanging on it.

Emily could see her blue one. It was next to Beast's.

His was green and red.

It was the best in the class.

"Now," said Ms. Rooney. She smiled. "It's time for everyone to tell about his secret December person."

Matthew raised his hand. "My secret December person is my best friend," he said. "It's Beast."

Beast held his magnifying glass up to his eye. "And my secret person is my friend Matthew."

Matthew clapped his hand to his head. "I never guessed," he said.

Emily stood up. "My secret December person," she said slowly, "is Jill Simon. She's a very nice girl."

Jill smiled. Today Jill was wearing her red ribbons again. But she had only three braids.

"Hey," Dawn Bosco said.

Emily looked over at her.

"I thought I was your secret December person," Dawn said.

Emily shook her head.

"But you baked those gorgeous cookies for me," Dawn said.

"Yes," Emily said. "Because of the fire-truck line."

"Oh," Dawn said. "That was very nice."

"Yes," Emily said again.

"Then next year," Dawn said, "maybe you'll let me get ahead of you."

"Maybe," Emily said. "But I'm not sure yet."

Jill Simon stood up. "I had a very special secret person," she said. "Her name is—"

Emily looked at her.

"Her name is," Jill said again, "Emily Arrow."

"Wow," Emily said. "Thank you for the red crayon."

"You're welcome," Jill said.

"And thank you for Uni's cover," Emily said.

Jill laughed. She pulled at her braids. "I used one of my red hair ribbons."

Emily finished the last of her potato *latke*.

She looked up at the Christmas tree. Then she

looked at her macaroni box. Jill was going to love
it.

She leaned over to Dawn again. "How about
coming over to my house tomorrow? You and Jill
and Beast and Matthew."

"All right," Dawn said.

Emily looked out the window.

It had started to snow.

"Jingle bells," Emily sang under her breath.

Next to her Dawn started to sing too.

Emily sang a little louder.

"Let's all sing," said Ms. Rooney.

Emily looked at Dawn. It was December. She
sang a little softer.

Then Dawn sang a little softer too.

"Lovely," said Ms. Rooney.

Emily smiled. She thought it was lovely too.

Esther Hautzig

RICHES

illustrated by Donna Diamond

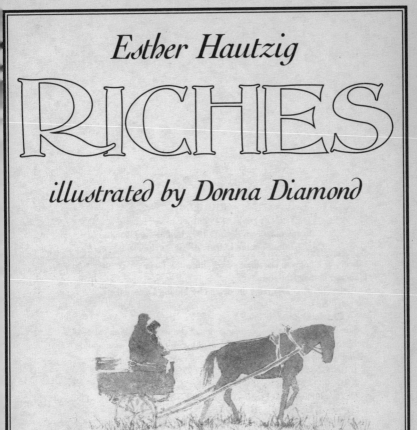

A CHARLOTTE ZOLOTOW BOOK

HarperTrophy
A Division of HarperCollinsPublishers

RICHES

Text copyright © 1992 by Esther Hautzig

Illustrations copyright © 1992 by Donna Diamond

Printed in the U.S.A. All rights reserved.

Library of Congress Cataloging-in-Publication Data

Hautzig, Esther Rudomin.

  Riches / Esther Hautzig ; illustrated by Donna Diamond.

    p. cm.

  "A Charlotte Zolotow book."

  Summary: After following the advice of the wisest rabbi in the area, a rich storekeeper discovers that giving of himself is better than merely giving money.

  ISBN 0-06-022259-X. — ISBN 0-06-022260-3 (lib. bdg.)

  ISBN 0-06-440550-8 (pbk.)

  [1. Conduct of life—Fiction.   2. Money—Fiction.   3. Jews—Fiction.] I. Diamond, Donna, ill.   II. Title.

PZ7.H289Ri 1992   89-26904

[Fic]—dc20   CIP

                                         AC

First Harper Trophy edition, 1994.

ONE

A long time ago a couple named Samuel and Chaya-Rivka lived in Antokol, a small town on the river Vilia. They were married for many, many years. Samuel and Chaya-Rivka raised two fine sons and a good daughter and they worked very hard side by side all their lives.

When Samuel and Chaya-Rivka reached three score and ten years of age they were considered a rich old couple. Their dry goods store was considered the best in their little corner of Eastern Europe. Samuel sold the best scythes, hoes, hammers, saws, axes and nails. Farmers, merchants and builders trusted him and came from all over the area to buy tools and farm implements from Samuel.

"Always buy the best you can and it will last you a lifetime," Samuel told his customers. And they did.

Chaya-Rivka stocked the prettiest fabrics, yarns and trimmings on the shelves of their store. Women from towns and villages near and far came to buy materials and buttons, threads and needles. Chaya-Rivka was always jolly and friendly and she did not stint a few extra centimeters when she measured out the goods.

She even gave an extra button to everyone who bought a dozen. "A baker's

dozen," she'd say, smiling, "even though you can't eat them!"

And they were always generous with their money. They gave food and clothing to the orphanage. They sent money to the old-age home in Antokol. They dropped silver coins into the cups of all the beggars on the street and those who came to their store.

But Samuel and Chaya-Rivka never had time to stop and visit at the orphanage or at the old-age home. They were too busy to speak to the beggars on the street or in the store. All Samuel and Chaya-Rivka had time for was work and more work.

ne evening, as they were tidying up the store, Samuel said to Chaya-Rivka, "Maybe it is time we stopped working? Soon it will be fifty years that we are married and have opened our store. Shouldn't there be more to life than hard work?"

"I would like to stay home and read holy books in peace and think about what I read without the bustle of the store."

Chaya-Rivka sighed as she rolled up the large bolts of fabric and put them on the shelf. "But hard work is most pleasing to the Almighty," she quietly added as she put the spools of thread into the glass case under the counter.

"Maybe you are right, dear wife. Hard work is pleasing to the Almighty. And I don't know what useful deed we can perform when we no longer work! Admire nature? Look at stars? I have no answers!"

Samuel pulled on his mustache and

looked away from Chaya-Rivka.

"I think I shall consult with the Gaon of Vilna, the wisest rabbi of all. I will go to him and seek his advice."

Chaya-Rivka was astonished. The Gaon of Vilna was the most revered of all rabbis in their region. Everyone respected him and followed his teachings. But she'd heard that the Gaon did not speak to strangers. He prayed and studied almost round the clock. People said he slept for only two hours out of every twenty-four. In half-hour periods! In an unheated room! And Samuel would go to seek the revered Gaon's advice on what he and she should do when they stopped working?

"Go to Vilna and see him," she nevertheless told Samuel. "Perhaps no matter is too small if it's done to please God as well as man."

THREE

Samuel came to the house of the Gaon of Vilna just before dusk. As always, he put on his prayer shawl to recite his prayers. When the prayers were over, Samuel remained in the shadows of the room and waited for the Gaon to take a respite from his studies. Finally the Gaon turned his head. Samuel quickly approached him.

"Rabbi, I am a stranger to you and yet I've come to ask you for a great favor."

The Gaon smiled. "Amongst us there are no strangers. Sit down, dear friend." He pointed to a chair and lit another candle on his table. "Do you have a place to spend the night? Do you need food or clothing?"

"No, Rabbi, I lack for nothing. I have a fine wife, good children, a comfortable home. We have a good business as well in Antokol."

"Why then did you come to me?" asked the Gaon.

"I need your counsel!" Samuel cried out. "My wife and I have worked hard all our lives. Now that we are old we want to stop. But what should we *do* that will be pleasing to the Almighty when we no longer work?"

The Gaon did not seem annoyed or surprised. He stroked his beard in silence and observed Samuel. At last he spoke.

"I think you should become a horse-and-cart driver in Antokol."

Samuel leaned across the table in astonishment. "It would be pleasing to the Almighty that I do the simplest work in our town? I don't need the money! I can't take away business from Jeremiah, who drives the horse and cart in Antokol!"

"You won't do it to earn money," the Gaon firmly replied. "Take your horse and cart onto deserted roads outside Antokol. Do not seek business in town."

"And my wife? What can she do? She says she'd like to stay at home and study prayer books in peace."

"Good," the Gaon replied. "Then she should stay home and study. Far better that she should use her mind on books than on idle chatter."

Samuel and the Gaon looked intently at each other. At last Samuel got up.

"If you believe that this is what we should do, then we shall do it, for you are the wisest rabbi in all the world!"

"There is no one wisest rabbi in the world! Everyone is a little wise and a little foolish. Sometimes more, sometimes less."

The Gaon reached for his books and moved the candles closer.

"Come back after you've driven your horse and cart for three months, except on Sabbath of course! I want to know how you've fared."

FOUR

Samuel returned to Antokol and told Chaya-Rivka of the Gaon's advice. She too was astonished.

"After all the years you've spent as a busy and successful storekeeper, after all of that you should become a simple horse-and-cart driver?"

Since Chaya-Rivka was not only a smart and industrious woman but a pious one as well, she did not argue very long

with the Gaon's edict. And she was
pleased that the Gaon had told Samuel
that she could stay at home and study
books.

*Perhaps by studying the books I'll learn
about wise rabbis' teachings and understand
their advice*, she thought.

Samuel and Chaya-Rivka spent the entire summer showing their children and grandchildren how to run the store so their customers would remain happy. They checked their stock. They paid their bills and collected what was owed them. Everything was set in order.

FIVE

Whenall the holidays—Rosh
Hashanah, Yom Kippur
and Succoth—were over,
Samuel bought a horse and cart. From
that day on Samuel and his light-brown
mare bumped along deserted, rutted
roads outside Antokol.

Sometimes Samuel glimpsed farmers
digging up the last of their summer
gardens. Other days he saw nothing but

trees in the red-and-golden glory of fall colors. Sometimes he stopped his cart and just looked across the fields, up into the sky at birds in flight, at forests. In years past he had seen these same trees but had no time to stop. He had had no time to admire nature.

When he came home, Chaya-Rivka would often eagerly inquire: "What happened today?"

"Nothing happened," Samuel would reply slowly. "But there was a birch tree with leaves that were bright yellow against its white bark. It shone like a beam of sunlight, even though the day was cloudy."

Chaya-Rivka was surprised. Never did Samuel tell her how a birch tree looked, and he'd seen them all his life!

SIX

When the weather became chilly and windy, Chaya-Rivka asked with great concern, "Couldn't you stay at home on this cold and blustery day?"

"No," Samuel replied. "The Gaon said that I should drive out every day, except on Sabbath of course, for three months. And so I shall."

Chaya-Rivka knew that it was useless to argue with her husband. She gave him an extra-warm sweater to wear beneath

his coat. She wound a large and soft scarf around his neck.

"Come back early if you get chilled. Hot broth and tea are always ready for you here at home!"

"Stop fussing over me, dear wife," Samuel said with a big smile.

"I'm not fussing, Samuel! I am taking care of you, as I said I would when we were married nearly fifty years ago!" Chaya-Rivka's eyes sparkled. "God be with you today and always," she called out as he drove away.

The countryside was deserted as Samuel drove up and down the roads outside Antokol. The trees were nearly bare, the wind blew strongly. Suddenly he noticed a small figure on the horizon.

"Giddyup," he called gently to his mare. The horse broke into a trot. When Samuel came closer, he found that it was

an old woman, bent under a heavy sack
slung on her back.

"Peace to you, my friend," he called
out. "Your load looks heavy. What's in
it?" The woman put down her heavy
sack. Samuel saw that she was crippled
and frail.

"I've been to the potato fields around
here. I've dug up potatoes that farmers
left behind, buried deep inside the earth.
They're in my sack." She pointed to it
with pride.

Samuel frowned. The potatoes farmers left in the ground were always small, half frozen and spoiled.

Perhaps I should give her a few rubles to buy good potatoes?

Something stopped him.

She is not a beggar and does not ask for anything of me. And she looks pleased with her findings.

"Would you like me to drive you home in my cart?" he asked.

"Oh, yes, I would," the old woman replied. "But unless you are the Prophet Elijah in disguise I cannot go with you! Ordinary cart drivers must be paid for their trouble, and I haven't a kopeck on me."

She bent down to lift her sack.

"Well, I'm not the Prophet Elijah," Samuel said with a smile, "but tell me where you live."

24

"I live near Lubtch, with two cats I found in the alley," she replied, "about two kilometers from here."

"I'm on my way to Lubtch right now," Samuel quickly said, "and since I'm going there anyway, I'll be glad to have you ride with me."

"Well, if you are going that way, I will ride with you. Even if you're not Elijah!"

She flung the sack into the cart and climbed in. Samuel clicked his tongue and the cart lurched along the bumpy road.

The woman hummed a song about Elijah, a song every child and grown-up knew, and looked slyly at Samuel. Samuel hummed companionably and smiled until they reached her hut outside of Lubtch.

"Oh, thank you, thank you," the woman said with a big smile. "Now I'm not a bit tired. I can roast potatoes for my cats and me, and we'll have a fine meal tonight."

She looked so happy and proud that Samuel was glad he did not offer her money. He felt glad about what he'd done for her instead.

As he rode back to Antokol, Samuel thought how nice it would be to tell his Chaya-Rivka that someone thought he was the Prophet Elijah doing good deeds in disguise! Just like in the books she was reading every day.

SEVEN

Soon snow covered the ground. The air was bitter cold and winds blew ever harder all day long. Still Samuel drove out each morning, after prayers, into the countryside, just as the Gaon had told him to do. The three months weren't over and Samuel was determined to keep his promise.

Just as he left Antokol one day, he noticed a young boy carrying a baby in his arms, walking slowly down the road.

He wore a threadbare jacket. The baby
was wrapped in a flimsy blanket.

"Where are you going, my child?"
Samuel called out.

"To Volokumpia, to find my family," he
answered hesitantly. "My brother is ill
and getting worse."

"But Volokumpia is far away! You
cannot walk there! And carrying a sick
baby! Where are your parents?"

"They are both dead," the boy

whispered, and began to weep. "Father died last spring. We came a short while ago to Antokol, so my mother could find work. Then she got ill and died also. We have no family here and I want to go to Volokumpia to find my aunt and uncle. They will help us!" Large tears rolled down the boy's cheeks.

"I'm going to Volokumpia on business, my child," Samuel quickly said. "I'll take you there and we'll find your relatives."

He got down and helped the young boy and his baby brother climb into the cart. Samuel covered them with straw and hay, and he wound his warm scarf around the baby.

"Are you a Lamed-Vovnik?" the young boy whispered to Samuel. "Can you be one of the thirty-six just men who live under humble guises and perform good deeds?"

Samuel patted the children with a happy smile. The mare took off as soon as Samuel tugged the reins and they sped along to Volokumpia.

Samuel did not return home till very late that night. His eyelashes and mustache had turned white with frost. His hands and feet were numb from the icy wind. Chaya-Rivka was beside herself with worry when she met him at the door.

"What happened to you, dear husband?" she cried out.

"I helped two orphans find their aunt and uncle all the way in Volokumpia." Samuel patted Chaya-Rivka's shoulder. "The older one asked me if I was a Lamed-Vovnik," he added shyly.

"Who knows? I've read a lot about them lately and maybe you are!" Chaya-Rivka answered proudly.

EIGHT

Only two weeks were left before Samuel was to go back to Vilna to see the Gaon. Although the roads were covered with snow and the weather cruel, he still went out each morning with his horse and cart.

One Friday afternoon, while the snow glistened in the sun, Samuel met Gabriel, the beggar, who sang each day on Antokol streets and in the marketplace. Samuel often dropped coins into his tin cup, but he never had time to stop and talk, or comment on his songs.

Gabriel trudged along the road, feeling his way with his stick, for he was nearly blind.

"Peace to you, my friend," Samuel called out.

"And to you," replied Gabriel, squinting into Samuel's direction. "Who may you be?"

"Oh, just a horse-and-cart driver, going home for Sabbath. And where are you going?"

"I'm going home to Nemenchin for Sabbath, too, but I'm afraid I won't get there before sundown. My eyesight is getting worse. I misjudged the time of day."

The beggar looked in the direction of the setting sun.

Samuel got off his cart. He put his hands on Gabriel's shoulders.

"You'll never get to Nemenchin on time for Sabbath. Come home with me, my friend. We'll welcome Sabbath together."

Gabriel peered into Samuel's face.

"You look like Samuel, the rich storekeeper. But it cannot be; rich storekeepers don't ask beggars to their homes for Sabbath."

Samuel did not reply. He helped Gabriel get into his cart. When Samuel and Gabriel arrived home, Chaya-Rivka was already waiting at the door. She looked at Samuel and then at Gabriel.

"I've brought an honored guest for Sabbath," Samuel quickly said. He helped Gabriel inside the room, where the table was set and candles were lit. The house was filled with all the good smells of Sabbath cooking.

"What is your name, dear host?" the beggar asked. "Your house is warm and it smells of foods cooked by rich folk."

"My name is Samuel, and my wife's is Chaya-Rivka."

"So you are the rich shopkeeper after all," the beggar cried out.

"What of it? I'm just a man, like you!" Samuel answered with spirit.

They had a good Sabbath eve together. They enjoyed the food, sang hymns and talked of things they knew.

"You must come to welcome the Sabbath with us each Friday and stay the night. We have room for you and a soft bed with down blankets. Tomorrow we'll go to synagogue together and say the Havdallah prayers here as well," Samuel told Gabriel.

"Yes, yes," Chaya-Rivka said. Gabriel happily accepted.

NINE

The three months were over. It was time for Samuel to see the Gaon of Vilna.

Again Samuel waited a long time in the shadows of the Gaon's synagogue. When at last Samuel faced the Gaon, the rabbi quietly asked:

"Well, Samuel, how did matters go with your wife? Did she read and study much?"

"Oh, yes, Gaon, she did. She has read legends about Elijah the Prophet, and

stories of the Lamed-Vovniks. She has knowledge she has never had before."

"That is good, and pleasing to the Almighty. And what did you accomplish?" the Gaon continued gently.

"Not much, I fear to say."

"Really?" the Gaon persisted. "Tell me what you saw."

Samuel recounted his trips on deserted roads. He described the beauty of nature, the changing seasons, cloud formations, falling snow and fields glistening in the sun.

"I never did have time to see God's

world in all its beauty before. But was that enough to please the Almighty?" Samuel peered anxiously into the Gaon's face.

"Seeing, really *seeing*, Samuel! That is pleasing to the Creator of the Universe. How many people do that in a lifetime?" The Gaon looked kindly at Samuel.

"And now tell me what you did," he continued.

"I took a crippled woman to her home in my horse and cart. She carried a heavy sack with potatoes she had dug up after the farmers finished their harvest." Samuel's face was creased with worry. "Maybe you know how bitter to the taste such potatoes are? But she looked so happy that she had found them! Should I have given her money to buy good potatoes instead?"

"Tell me more," the Gaon said, without answering Samuel's question.

"Well, I drove young orphans to Volokumpia to find their family." Samuel lowered his eyes. "Would it have been wiser and better in God's eyes had I given them money to ride the stagecoach?"

Samuel pulled nervously on his mustache before he went on speaking.

"And I asked Gabriel the beggar to my home when he was going to be late getting home for Sabbath one cold Friday afternoon, and I also asked him to spend every Sabbath with us for the rest of our days."

The Gaon sat very still and observed Samuel with great kindness.

"Tell me, Rabbi, should I have given Gabriel a generous donation instead, so he would not need to sing on the streets of Antokol and wait for coins to be put in his cup?"

"Samuel, my friend, you did right in all

three cases. To give of *yourself* and not of your money is God's special way of bestowing riches on the giver and the receiver."

The Gaon put his hands on Samuel's head.

"Go home to your dear wife. Pray each day, as always. Give charity, as ever. But also give of *yourself* whenever and wherever you can."

And Samuel went home a happy man. He told Chaya-Rivka what the Gaon had said. She was proud and happy, too.

For Samuel and Chaya-Rivka's fiftieth wedding anniversary, soon after the holiday of Passover, when all the spring planting was completed, their children and grandchildren and people from the entire area came to celebrate. The old

woman came bearing a delicious potato kugel. The young orphans came with their aunt and uncle, carrying a bouquet of flowers from the fields around Antokol. And Gabriel came too and sang a special song in honor of the celebration.